STORYTIME COLLECTION

STORYTIME COLLECTION

This book belongs to

_____

_____

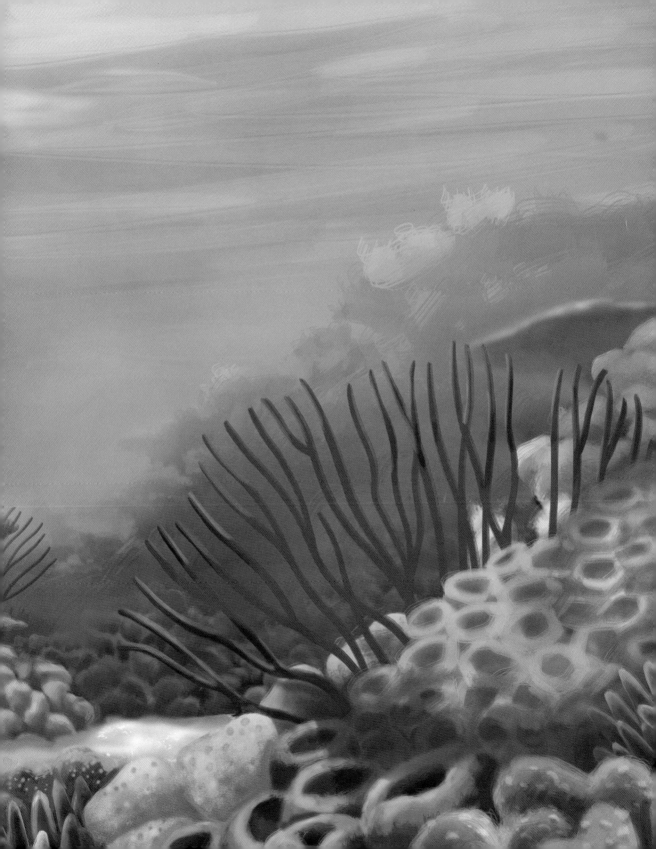

Autumn
Publishing

Published in 2018
by Autumn Publishing
Cottage Farm
Sywell
NN6 0BJ
www.igloobooks.com

GUA009 0718
2 4 6 8 10 9 7 5 3
ISBN 978-1-78810-991-8

Printed and manufactured in China

 STORYTIME COLLECTION

One day, at the edge of the Great Barrier Reef, a mother clownfish, called Coral, and a father clownfish, called Marlin, were talking about all the names they were going to give to their little eggs. "I like Nemo," said Coral.

Suddenly, a barracuda attacked and Marlin was knocked out cold. When he finally woke up, Coral was gone and only one of the eggs remained. "I promise I will never let anything happen to you, Nemo," said Marlin, cradling the tiny egg close to his body.

The next few years whizzed by and, before Marlin knew it, he was taking Nemo to his first day at school. Marlin kept fretting over Nemo and was worried about leaving him. "Don't worry," said Mr. Ray, Nemo's teacher, as he led the little fish away.

Not long after, Marlin found out the class were going to the Drop-off. This was the place where the barracuda had attacked his family. Worried for his only child, Marlin chased after them.

When Marlin had finally caught up with the class, he dragged Nemo away from the edge of the Drop-off. "You shouldn't be anywhere near here!" he cried.

Nemo, annoyed that his father would never let him do anything, was determined to show he could do what he wanted. So, he swam up to a boat bobbing on the surface and slapped it with his fin.

Feeling like he'd shown his dad he didn't
need to be looked after so much, Nemo swam
back down. Suddenly, a diver appeared and scooped
the little clownfish into a net. "Daddy! Help me!"
shouted Nemo, as the diver took him up to the surface.

"Nemo!" cried Marlin, who swam to the surface as fast as his fins would let him. But the boat was too quick for Marlin to follow, and was soon just a speck in the distance.

As it disappeared from view, the scuba mask worn by the diver fell into the ocean.

Marlin rushed to get help.

"Has anybody seen a boat?" he asked every
fish he saw, but no one cared. Then Marlin, furiously
swimming around, collided with a regal blue tang called Dory.
"I've seen a boat," she said. "Follow me!"

What Marlin didn't know was that Dory had a very bad memory.
Soon, she'd forgotten why Marlin was following her! "You got a
problem, buddy?" she asked the confused clownfish.

As Marlin started to swim away from Dory, he came face-to-face with
a great white shark called Bruce, who invited them both to a party.
Marlin and Dory had no choice but to agree.

Bruce took them to a sunken submarine to meet his two friends.
Marlin found out all three sharks were vegetarians. "Fish are friends,
not food!" they chanted together. As they spoke, Marlin noticed the
diver's mask and swam over to it.

As Marlin and Dory studied the mask, the strap snapped into Dory's nose. She bled a few drops of blood, which floated up into Bruce's nostrils. He wasn't a vegetarian any more…

"I'm having fish tonight!" cried Bruce. The hungry shark snapped and snarled, but Marlin and Dory just managed to escape.

Meanwhile, Nemo was suddenly dropped into strange
waters. All around him were plastic plants, a toy volcano
and invisible walls. Nemo was inside a fish tank!

As Nemo swam around the tank, he came across a friendly group of fish. They were delighted to meet someone from the open sea! Soon, a pelican, called Nigel, stopped by to visit, too.

Just then, the dentist appeared and shooed Nigel away, then told Nemo he was to be given as a present to his niece, Darla. "She's a fish-killer," declared Nemo's new friends.

Nemo panicked. "I have to get back to
my dad!" he cried. Backing away, the young
clownfish got sucked into the filter used to keep the tank clean.

Gill, the leader of the tank gang, went over to Nemo and showed
him how to escape safely. Soon, Nemo had wiggled free. "Perfect,"
said Gill, who knew the little fish was small enough to help with an
escape plan he had put together.

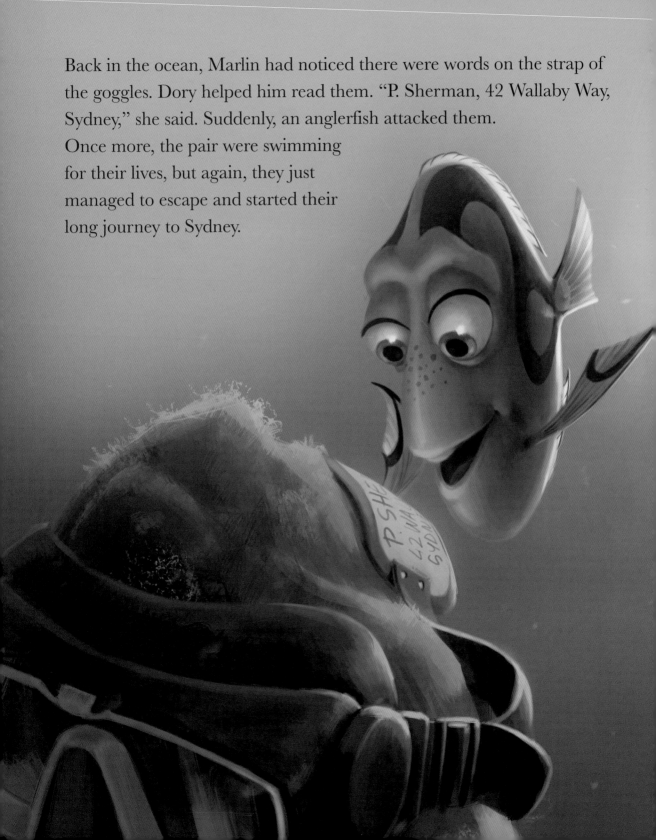

Back in the ocean, Marlin had noticed there were words on the strap of the goggles. Dory helped him read them. "P. Sherman, 42 Wallaby Way, Sydney," she said. Suddenly, an anglerfish attacked them. Once more, the pair were swimming for their lives, but again, they just managed to escape and started their long journey to Sydney.

Not knowing the way, Marlin and Dory quickly became lost. Eventually, they found a school of moonfish. "Any of you heard of Sydney?" Dory asked them.

"Follow the East Australian Current," they said. The moonfish then made themselves into the shape of an arrow to show the correct way to go.

Back in the tank, Nemo was talking to Gill. He was curious about the fish's damaged fin. "My first escape," explained Gill. "I was aiming for the toilet."

"The toilet?" asked Nemo.

"All drains lead to the ocean, kid," replied Gill.

Soon, it was time to put their escape plan into action!
Nemo was told to use a pebble to jam the filter that kept
the tank clean, but as the little fish tried, he was dragged
towards the spinning blades. Luckily, the tank gang
were able to pull him out just in time.
Unfortunately, for Nemo especially,
the escape plan had failed.

Meanwhile, Marlin and Dory were hitching a ride with a turtle called Crush along the East Australian Current. Marlin watched Crush encourage his son, Squirt, to be adventurous and have fun. "You so totally rock, Squirt!" cried Crush. Marlin started to wonder if he'd been too protective of Nemo.

Squirt wanted to know more about Marlin so, the clownfish told his story and soon it spread throughout the ocean. All sorts of animals began retelling the tale of how Marlin was looking for his son.

It wasn't long before news had reached Sydney, where Nigel the pelican heard everything. He flew straight to tell Nemo.

Nigel soon arrived at the fish tank.

"Your dad's been fighting the entire ocean looking for you," he told Nemo.

"My father?" asked Nemo. "Really?"

Nigel nodded enthusiastically and told Marlin's story. "Word is, he's headed this way to Sydney," added Nigel.

After hearing how brave his dad had been, Nemo jumped
into the filter again. He was determined to succeed this
time. He jammed the blades with a rock and, with a
CRUNCH and a CLANG, the filter stopped.
"You did it!" cried Gill.

Out in the ocean, Marlin and Dory said goodbye to the sea turtles. They headed for Sydney, but soon got lost in the murky waters. Suddenly, they came across a blue whale. Dory asked it the way to Sydney but, instead of answering, it sucked them both into its huge mouth!

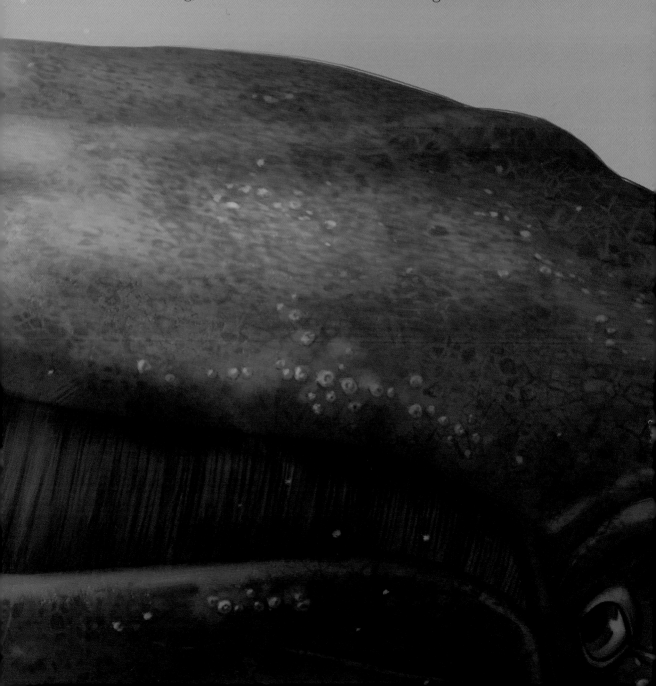

In the dentist's office, Gill and Nemo were admiring their handiwork.
"Will you look at that?" said Gill. "Filthy. Absolutely filthy."

The gang were swimming in green and slimy water.
Nothing in the tank was clean and the fish
couldn't have been happier.

"I've gotta clean the fish tank before Darla gets here," said the dentist. Gill's plan had worked! Nemo would be free before the little girl could take him away.

That night, the whale who'd swallowed Marlin and Dory pushed them out of its spout into... Sydney Harbour! Realising where they were, Marlin quickly started searching for the diver's boat, but couldn't find it.

In the morning, a pelican appeared and quickly scooped them up in its beak.

That same morning,
Nemo and his friends woke up.
Today was the day they'd escape to open water.
But there was one problem. The tank was already
clean! The dentist had installed a new, high-tech
filter while they wcre sleeping. "What are we gonna do about—" started
Nemo, but before he could finish, the dentist swept a plastic bag through
the water, picked Nemo up and lifted him out of the tank.

At that moment, Darla burst into the room, desperate for her new fish. However, Nemo had a plan. He decided to float belly-up in the water! Assuming he had died, the dentist hid the bag behind his back so Darla couldn't see.

Suddenly, Nigel flew in through the window! Marlin saw
Nemo floating belly-up and thought his son was dead!
"Nemo!" cried Marlin. Before he could say anything
more, the dentist grabbed Nigel and threw the pelican out
of the window, taking Marlin and Dory with him!

Hearing his father's voice, Nemo stopped playing dead. "Fishy," said Darla, who saw Nemo was alive. Suddenly, she started shaking the bag. "Why are you sleeping?" cried Darla.

On his orders, the tank gang quickly launched Gill out of the toy volcano. The stream of water sent him high into the air and right on top of Darla's head. The little girl screamed and dropped Nemo's bag, which landed on the dentist's tray and burst open.

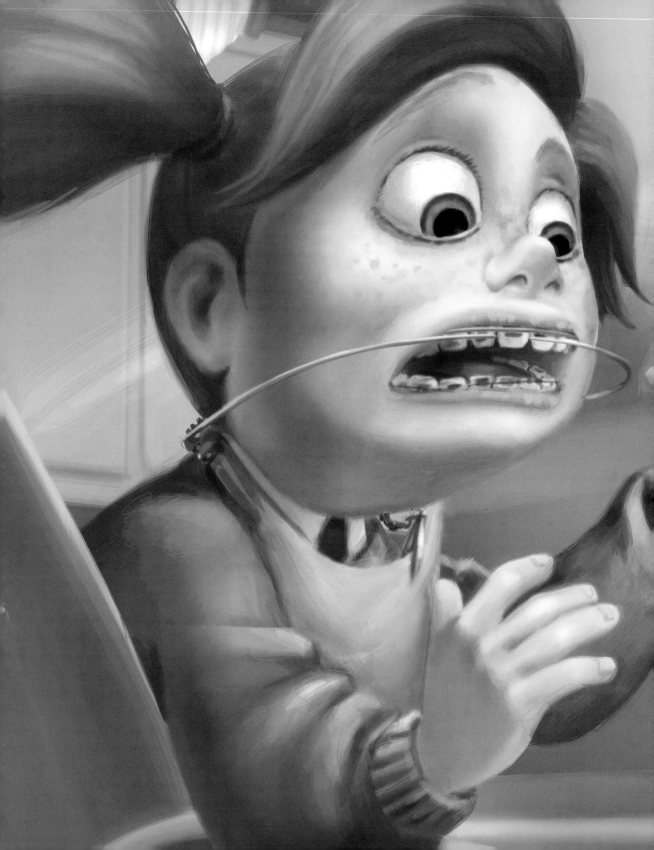

Gill then flipped himself onto the tray. "Tell your dad I said 'hi,'" he said, before smacking his tail against a dental mirror. Nemo was catapulted over Darla's snatching hands and into a plughole.

The little fish escaped down the drain.

"Is he going to be okay?" the rest of the tank gang asked Gill, who had been put back in the tank by the dentist.

"Don't worry," he replied. "All drains lead to the ocean."

Back in the harbour, Nigel put Marlin and Dory back in the ocean. All of them believed Nemo was dead. "I'm so sorry," said Nigel, before flying away.

Marlin was heartbroken. "It's over, Dory," he said, sadly. "We were too late. Nemo's gone and I'm going home now."

"No, you can't," said Dory. Marlin had become like family to her and she didn't want him to go. However, it was too late. Marlin had gone.

Not long after, Nemo
shot up through a pipe and
into the ocean where he bumped
into Dory. At first, she wasn't
sure who he was, but suddenly, Dory
remembered everything! The regal blue tang
was so excited to have found the little clownfish
at last. She knew they had to find Marlin, but had
no idea where he'd gone. Luckily, some crabs knew.
"He went to the fishing grounds," they said.

Dory and Nemo swam
as quickly as their fins
would let them and soon
found Marlin. "Nemo!"
cried Marlin, so happy to see
his son again.

Suddenly, a large net swept up
Dory along with a large school
of grouper fish!

Nemo bravely swam into the net.
Remembering what Gill had taught him,
Nemo said to his dad, "Tell all the fish to swim
down." So, Marlin did as his son said, and soon all
the fish were swimming down. Such was the strain
against the rope, that it soon broke open and all the
fish, including Dory, escaped.

Once the groupers had swum away, Marlin found his son pinned beneath the heavy net. "Nemo?" said Marlin, worriedly. Then, to his enormous relief, his son's eyes fluttered open. He was going to be all right.

Marlin finally realised that even though his son was very small, he was capable of doing very big things!

A few weeks later, Marlin had just dropped Nemo off at school. All Marlin's friends had come to see Nemo, too.

As everyone watched, Marlin gave his son a big hug. "Go have an adventure," said Marlin, who then watched Nemo swim off with the rest of the school.

THE END

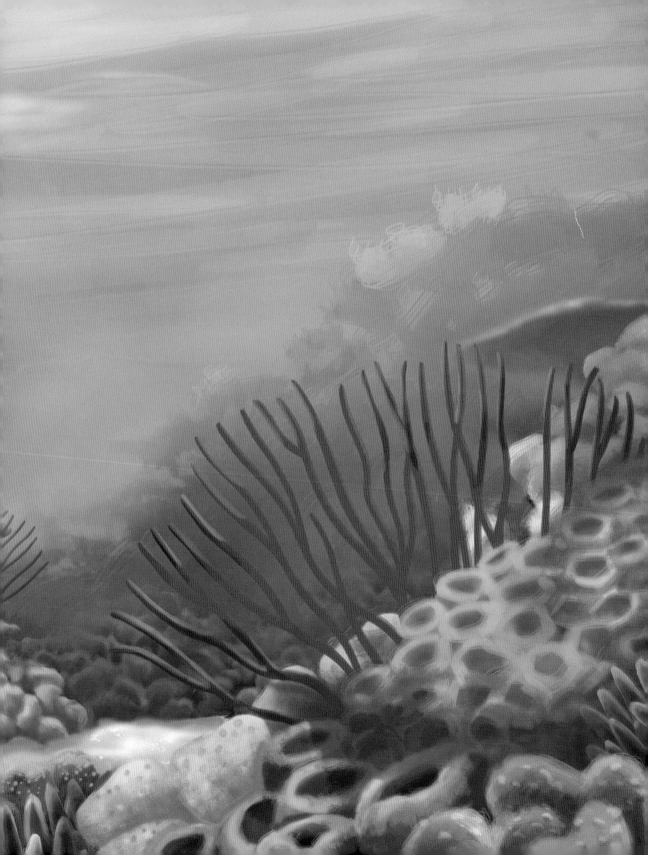

COLLECT THEM ALL!

With 7 more exciting titles to choose from, you'll want to complete your Storytime Collection!

Will Simba ever become king?

Will Rapunzel learn who she truly is?

Will Moana be able to save the ocean?

Can Anna and Elsa stop an eternal winter?

Will Mowgli defeat Shere Khan?

Will the Incredibles save the day?

Will Belle be able to break the curse?